CW00809037

ACT & VIST

At the beginning

The prequel (-1) to the series WHO IS VIST

Anka B. Troitsky

The Author asserts the moral right to be identified as the author of this work.

All rights reserved. No part of this publication may be reproduced or transmitted, in any form or otherwise, without the copyright owner's prior permission.

The cover art used also belongs to the Author. The characters and events in this book are completely fictitious. Any possible similarities are not intentional.

(This book contains scenes of violence)

Copyright © 2024 Anka B. Troitsky
Published in the UK by Greystone Consultancy LTD
ISBN: 978-1-7391959-7-7

To my incredible friends, whose unwavering support and belief in me made this journey a reality, this book is for you.

I am grateful to my partner Richard for his support and encouragement.
Also, to my editor, Andrew Hodges, The Narrative Craft.

Contents

Epigraph

"You have no right to a prize. You have a right to earn it."

Engraved on a young athlete's medal. 1993

1. 16/12/3406

I hate it when blood gets in my eyes, especially when it's not mine. It's a good thing Lez seized the initiative and dropped like a sack at the feet of the Cruiser who had clearly decided to finish me off. The Cruiser, a skinny but strong guy, tripped over nearly one hundred kilograms of my love, got tangled in his cassock, and fell onto my blade with a cry of horror. I felt, rather than heard, steel scraping against his ribs. He died, impaled on my bayonet as if on a spit, red liquid pouring from his mouth.

I jumped back, wiped my face, and looked around. What if help arrived? But no, it seemed he was truly alone. The alley of the abandoned Champlain quarter of Vermont was empty. Two crows, disturbed by the fight, returned and perched on the remains of a drainpipe that had come off the cornice.

Lez stood up, rubbing his side. "Damn, their iron boots. Why do they wear such heavy clothes nowadays? I didn't have to when I was a Moon Brother," he complained loudly.

"Because these unfortunate members of the Moses Movement only experience pleasure when they take all this off before bed. Rumour has it they feel so good then that they don't even need sex," I said, pushing the corpse with my foot to free my weapon.

"What are we going to do with the body? Min Jee, my flower, I really don't want to dig a grave or collect wood scraps for cremation," Lez grumbled, searching for his knife, which the Cruiser had knocked out of his hands.

I searched the dead Cruiser. "We'll leave him. You told me that brothers believe you must care for the soul, not the body. They will find him. His corpse will be turned into Angel Flesh and packed with the rest of the emergency provisions."

"Oh … don't remind me of that innovation." Lez paused, then added, "Disgusting!"

"Do you happen to remember if there are any secret pockets in these cassocks of theirs?" I stood up to my full height and looked at Lez, my expression feigning hope.

He burst out laughing and showed me the knife he had found. "Mooners don't have them, but the followers of Moses carry their valuables in the sewn-up fold of their sleeves."

He leaned over and felt the Cruiser's wide sleeves rolled into broad folds. With the knife, he ripped open the sky-blue fabric and pulled out a tube of flexible plastic tied with thread. He handed the tube to me.

"Here, Min. I hope this *is* what you were looking for."

I unrolled the thin plastic and saw two children's faces in the photograph – a boy and a girl, both about fourteen years old, smiling. The boy's head was shaved, but the girl had luxurious copper-red curls. Anyone could see they were twins. They had the same freckled noses and green eyes. It was hard to believe these were not ordinary children but the latest generation of loaders.

"AI imaging?" Lez asked, looking over my shoulder.

"Not this time. It's them. Let's leave here before the Cruiser's patrol comes through."

2. 16/12/3406

We arrived late at The Lord's Hand; of course, our room had been ransacked. Bags of food and Lez's new shoes had disappeared. He helped me move the massive bed away from the wall, then went to argue with the owner of this cheapest, busiest hotel in the city. I kneeled where the bed had been, took a screwdriver out of the tool case, and lifted the floorboard. Relieved, I pulled out a bag from this temporary cache. It contained a zapper – my zero-point-energy wrist gun – and a field terminal. In a minute, I connected to the MESH, banned by the new government. The city had been without electricity for a year, so I powered the terminal from my wrist gun, which converted energy from its non-living surroundings. Immediately, the light from the dozen candles burning on the table noticeably blurred. I had about twenty minutes before the signal of this encrypted communication would be detected, and the Moon Cruisers arrived.

I first scanned the photo of the two children and saved it in my Intersafe. Now I could access it from anywhere in the Solo System. A low-power energy beam from the zapper turned the piece of thin plastic into a small black drop in a second. It immediately cooled down, and I blew it off the table. Well, that's done. The last tangible image the Cruisers could identify the surviving twin with was destroyed. Now it would be harder for them to search, especially since the survivor should be in their late thirties. I updated my journal and replayed the video I made a few years ago.

I recalled how, in the festive crowd near the Academy of Sciences, I had seen a profile I had studied well and could not believe my eyes. Back then, I was a simple reporter for the MESH News and did not know the Cruisers would seize power on Earth a few years later. I raised the camera above my head and thought, could Lez be right? Had the boy survived? The profile of the shaved head was clearly visible on the screen for a few seconds. Then, this person in the space station coverall turned around and walked away. I almost dropped the camera. Only half of his head was shaved, and on the opposite side was shoulder-length copper hair, an unruly strand falling over one eyebrow. This discovery distracted me so much that I did not examine the face as I would have. I only remember that it wasn't beautiful, in my opinion. I like sharp angles and a heavy jaw with stubble, like Lez's. This face was too calm and sad, like that of a poet or a philosopher. I didn't know if I would ever meet this guy . . . or this girl, but I would not be surprised if they rarely smile now. Maybe, in that photo, they smiled for the last time.

From behind the door, my husband's booming voice could be heard from below through the stairwell: "I'm not asking for my money back. I still have to sleep here tonight, but your oversight will cost you the price of my shoes and plenty of food for the long road."

He raised his voice deliberately. This meant the first squad had passed through the street. I turned off and hid the equipment under the floor. The thick candles flared up again, but they looked like they had been burning for twenty hours, not twenty minutes. Lez came in and locked the door. We put the bed back in place and undressed; then there was a knock on the door.

In my lace nightgown, I opened the

door wider so the mountain of muscular flesh on the bed could be seen.

Lez sat up and growled. "What? Did you bring money for shoes? Praise the Lord!" The hotel owner stood in the doorway, two Cruisers in short brown cassocks there beside him. "We need to search the room," one armed with a sledgehammer said, and entered.

I squealed as high as I could, jumped onto the bed, and pulled the covers over my head. I felt under the pillow for Lez's knife and gripped the handle tightly, just in case we had to use the element of surprise.

"Where have you both been for the last twenty minutes, and what have you been doing?" the second Cruiser asked.

My husband stood up to his height before the rather burly Cruiser and said, "I just spent half an hour complaining to this man about the lousy security at this hotel." He pointed his fingers at the owner. "And now I'm about to have a hot night with this exotic babe," he added, pointing at me.

Above the covers, all they could see now were my eyes and tousled hair.

"That's true." The owner nodded, not crossing the threshold. "This man has already been robbed today."

"What do you mean, already?" The first Cruiser stepped towards him. "We are looking for rebels and blasphemers who violate the Lord's commandments - *don't dare enter the Lord's abode*. Which of your guests did you see with a computer and other abominations?"

"I didn't see—" the owner began, but then a shot of an ancient weapon and the screams of several people rang out at once from the next room. Apparently, the search there was going even worse. The Cruisers only had time to peer into the corners before running out of the room. The owner, with a doomed look, apologised and closed the door. My husband and I looked at each other.

"These two didn't recognise me," he mused.

"We didn't have to break noses and run off through the window this time," I said.

"Too bad," Lez said, chuckling, "I love watching these mystics fall face down in front of you like you're a goddess. It turns me on."

He pulled the blanket off me and sank his mouth into mine. I grabbed his wrists to hold him back, enjoying the feeling of him overpowering me. A minute later, my nightgown was in tatters. People were screaming and running outside the door, something was crashing and breaking behind the walls, and amid this chaos, in our room with the candles almost burned out, the shadows of our bodies danced on the walls.

3. 17/12/3406

While you use your imagination, let me introduce ourselves. I bet you can picture us most vividly right now.

This thirty-eight-year-old athletic woman with straight black hair and phoenix eyes is me. My name is Min Jee Prosser. Four years younger than me, this Scandinavian giant currently between my thighs is my husband, Lezoraz Prosser.

Lez and I never imagined that our lives would become so intertwined with a mission that felt larger than ourselves, a mission that had taken root in the ruins of our dying world.

Eight years ago, we were different people. I was just a journalist, curious and naive, chasing stories without fully understanding the darkness I would uncover.

Lez was an ex-Cruiser, a former member of the very sect responsible for the loader genocide. We used to be on opposite sides of a war, which neither of us had truly chosen, but life had other plans for us.

The loaders were a mystery I had grown up hearing about, tales spun by my father late at night that seemed too fantastical to be true. He spoke of them as humanity's last hope, as beings capable of unimaginable feats thanks to the technologies embedded within them. They could store entire archives in their heads. By touching another person's head, they could absorb not only their skills and memory but their conciseness, too. They were designed to survive the inconceivable and carry humanity's knowledge and skills forward if Earth fell. But instead of becoming our salvation, they became the targets of a new religious zealotry. The Cruisers, fanatics who saw the loaders as abominations, hunted them down until it was believed none were left.

When the last loader family was obliterated on the orbital station near KOSI (Kepler's Object of Special Interest), I was younger, just beginning my career. The event was shocking, but it wasn't until years later that I learned someone might have survived. This revelation became an obsession. I couldn't let it go or shake the feeling that if one loader was still alive, it was my duty to find him . . . or her. Perhaps it was just a hope that I could save something of our world by saving them.

Lez's journey was different. He had been a believer but also a man of conviction who saw the world in black and white. Disillusionment inevitably crept in, and when he narrowly survived his disassociation from the sect, he saw the world with new eyes. During this time, we met – two people shaped by different experiences but bound by a shared understanding of what was at stake. Over the years, our relationship became one forged in the fires of our shared mission. We became warriors for a cause we believed in more deeply than anything else.

Our path now leads us to a place that once symbolised hope for humanity – the facility where the Object mission trained colonists to fly through wormholes. There, we hope to meet someone by the name of Kir Vendy, a former assistant to the renowned scientist Vatslav Maiser. He was one of the few who truly understood the loaders' potential. If anyone can help us find the last surviving loader, that person is Kir. The journey has been long and the risks are immense, but we're ready. Whatever it takes, we'll find the loader and ensure that the legacy of those hunted can still shape the future of our species.

4. 18/12/3406

We managed to leave Vermont without incident. Our route passed through the ruins of Montreal and then across the desert to Lake Mistassini. This journey did not promise anything pleasant, but this desert was the only reason the Cruisers did not reach the third and last "Resort of Hope." Or rather, what was left of it. In 3390, I was in Detroit writing an article about that resort at Christmas, when Les and I met. I remember him sitting on one of the carousel horses, which creaked pitifully under him. I wondered why a huge adult man was celebrating a children's holiday. He said that when he was a child, his parents forbade him from meeting with the children of blasphemers for the traditional exchange of gifts. Soon, it will be Christmas Day again, a holiday almost forgotten since not many children are left on Earth. But I will think of something for my beloved "big boy."

We walked over a long bridge in the ruins with no water beneath it. The broad rivers were long gone. We looked for the least destroyed house for the night, but the city was not as empty as we had hoped. It was already getting dark when we found a street with tall apartment blocks on both sides.

"Look," Lez said, nodding at the house to our right.

Four windows on the top floor were without glass, covered with brown cloth and boarded up with plywood. Faint light leaked through the lower cracks from inside. A satellite wouldn't see it, but it was exposed from below.

I turned my eyes to the opposite side of the street. The windows there looked like the empty eye sockets of Old Believers crucified and hanged by Cruisers in Jericho.

"We should not walk openly under the windows," I said quietly. "Let's go over there."

We headed left and turned the corner, finding the back entrance to a large apartment building. This type of architecture was built after the first big drought. The houses looked like huge hotels or malls because the ground floors were not residential. The huge halls were like indoor squares, with shops and eateries along the perimeter, mostly run by the residents themselves. There, mini green parks were full of people, and birds sang in aviaries while the wind outside carried sand and dust between buildings. Now, of the wild birds, only crows and other scavengers remained. Of the plants, only giant trees or very small farmed flora had survived.

On the building's upper floors, there

were abandoned flats, but there was no point in looking for anything valuable. If there were people here, they would have found everything long ago. So we went along the ground floor. Through its enfilades, we could go all the way to the end of the block and, from there, enter another similar building. This way, I thought, we would pass by the inhabitants unnoticed.

However, I was wrong.

It was pitch-black inside, but we could travel in the darkest hours with night vision goggles. Yet, fatigue overcame us, and we had to stop for a rest. At the end of the building, we went up to the first floor and found an empty flat with nothing but bare walls and a broken door. What used to be a kitchen was almost intact and close enough to the entrance. We decided to spend the night there.

Lez untied the blankets, and as always, I

found a loose tile on the floor in the corner and lifted it to create a hiding place underneath. You never know. When I stuck my hand into the hole to check for enough room for my most valuable terminal – a device for MESH access – I felt a rectangular object inside. The room was dark, so I lit a match to see what I hadn't seen since we landed on the continent: a book! And not just any book, but a novel by the three Mattomere brothers, banned by the Cruisers – the second volume of *You, as Your Worst Enemy*. I couldn't think of a better Christmas present for Lez. What a lucky find! In addition, I no longer doubted the safety of the hiding place. I hid the book and the terminal in this makeshift safe and covered the slab with trash and dust blown into the apartment through the broken windows.

We didn't start a fire, but we heated two soup cans from the last hotel's kitchen with my zapper and scooped the contents directly out of the cans.

We usually took turns sleeping in such conditions, but Lez and I couldn't fall asleep for a long time despite our fatigue. I kept thinking about how happy he would be with the book. So we lay there, theorising who might still live in these ruins: Cruiser agents, Thieves or vagrants. We couldn't see the stars through the windows because of the dust clouds, but I could easily imagine them since I had seen them as a child.

Suddenly, I heard a faint rustling sound. Lez froze and put a finger to my lips. The sound grew louder, more distinct. It was the unmistakable shuffle of footsteps. We were being followed or tracked.

We got up as quietly as possible, put the goggles back on, took cover by both sides of the doorway, and peered out. Two people, ragged and gaunt, were timidly shuffling down the corridor towards us. I nodded to Lez, and he barked in his scary voice, "Stop! Not one step further."

The couple stopped and stared fearfully at the doorway. Perhaps this man and woman were travellers like us, looking for a room more or less protected from the night wind. The woman held a bunch of glimreed stalks in her hands, glowing dimly but enough to light their way. Their faces looked hollow, their eyes filled with fear and suspicion. We stepped out onto the broad landing to meet them. They stared at us, unmoving, as if expecting the worst.

"We are not hostile," Lez said, raising his hands slowly. "We're passing through these ruins, too. But I'm afraid you must find a different room for tonight."

The man, older than us and with a

greying beard, asked, "Who are you?"

"Wanderers," I replied. "We're heading to the desert."

The old man's eyes widened. "Why?"

"We're looking for Lake Mistassini," Lez said. "We heard it might still be safe, and the lake still has some water."

The old man relaxed, then laughed bitterly. "Safe? There's no safe place left. Not from the Cruisers and not from the weather. And as for water . . . that's just a rumour."

A woman, clutching a glowing bundle to her chest, stepped forward. "Please, can you help us? We haven't eaten for days."

I looked at Lez. We had little to offer, but we couldn't just say no. "We'll give you a couple of cans and a pack of croutons," I said, pointing back to the flat where we had camped. "It's not much, but it's all we can spare."

As I stepped back, the woman dropped the glimreed, which fell on the dusty floor with a dry rustle. She was now holding an old-fashioned zapper, pointing it at Lez, while the man lifted a hand with what looked like a bottle containing liquid and a wick.

"We will take it all, thank you very much," he said. "You will be spared if you just leave your things with us and walk out of here."

I pulled back my long sleeve and pointed my fist at the woman. On my wrist, my zapper looked like a watch with a cylindrical ray pointer.

"Can you tell the difference?" I asked her, noticing that her hands had started to shake. "Mine might be smaller than yours, but it works, and yours is missing a little light above the blade."

"And I wonder how you'll light that thing," Lez added.

There was little convertible energy at night, but my weapon had a few charges left. However, I could see that their zapper didn't have a converter at all, and the liquid inside the bottle was probably just rainwater. In the past, they may have managed to scare many people who didn't pay attention to details.

Thieves. Unfortunately, they usually come in dozens. This couple, too, were not alone. Several dark figures rushed towards us from all corridors and staircases. I zapped three before they got too close and extended my sharpened lance while Lez worked with his axe and knife. Clearly, these strangers had the advantage of numbers and knowledge of the surroundings in this dark place. It was just the two of us, armed with slightly superior weapons and skills. Plus, Lez was much better nourished and trained. He was hacking in all directions, but these people were like acrobats, dodging him six times out of ten. Out of the corner of my eye, I saw a man with an old knitted hat on his head sneak up on Lez from behind. I yanked the spear out of the torso of the enemy I had just defeated, stabbed it into the rotten floor, and used it as a pole as I ran along the wall. My heel struck the scoundrel on the hat, and he fell. I noticed that a woman ran into our room in the chaos and carried out our blankets with our belongings hastily wrapped in them.

The bottle in the man's hands turned out to be filled with a flammable mixture, not water. I didn't see where or how he lit the fuse, but I did notice the bottle flying towards us from the doorway of one of the apartments, tracing a bright arc in the air. Oh, he shouldn't have done that.

"Fire in the hole!" Lez shouted to me, and he leaped behind a square column. The flame flared up about three metres from me, but I rushed towards it instead of retreating. My converter activated immediately, absorbing the heat and light of the fire, and the flame quickly extinguished.

This sudden influx of energy was enough to charge my zapper for five more shots. I aimed and fired with precision, each shot slicing through the air and hitting its mark. Five Thieves fell, cut in half by the beam, their screams abruptly silenced. Lez re-emerged from behind the column, his eyes scanning the remaining threats. He nodded at me, and we both knew this fight wasn't over.

The number of desperate attackers did not decrease - on the contrary. I punched another Thief in the face, felt a weary pain in my arm, and realised we were losing this battle.

Suddenly, a strange sound rang out, like a balloon bursting, and the Thieves began to cover their faces with their hands. They stopped fighting; some tried to turn around and run, while others fell to their knees before collapsing and remaining still. I felt my limbs weaken, and my eyes faded to black. The last thing I heard was Lez's cough as I fell beside him, my body collapsing like a marionette with its strings cut.

5. 20/12/3406

When I woke up, the light burning through my eyelids told me it was daytime. I could hear Lez breathing heavily beside me, a cough rasping deep in his chest. I tried to reach out, to touch him and let him know I was there, but my limbs refused to obey.

Another few hours must have passed.

I drifted in and out of consciousness, my mind struggling to grasp anything to anchor me back to reality.

When I finally moved, it was in response to the faintest of sounds - a rustle, a distant hum. My body felt heavy and sluggish, as if I had been drugged. I forced my eyes open, blinking at the dust in the air. My head was throbbing, and my mouth was as dry as sandpaper.

I tried to sit up. Slowly, painfully, I rolled onto my side and took in my surroundings.

The place was unfamiliar.

We were no longer in the apartments of an abandoned building in Montreal's ruins. Instead, we lay on dry sand in the shade, with the arch of a large tunnel looming above us. We were lying by the mouth of this tunnel. Our belongings were nowhere to be seen.

Lez. My heart sank as I turned to look at him. He was lying on his back, his chest rising and falling in shallow breaths. Relief washed over me – he was alive.

"Lez," I croaked, my voice barely above a whisper. I crawled towards him, each movement an effort. "Lez, wake up."

He groaned, his eyelashes fluttering. When he saw me, his expression softened, but nausea quickly clouded his gaze. "Min . . . are you okay?"

I nodded, though I wasn't sure how true that was. "We've lost everything."

He cursed under his breath, trying to get up. I helped him as best I could, supporting his weight as he leaned against the tunnel wall.

We both looked around, trying to answer the most important question: where were we?

Lez peered into the tunnel, where darkness loomed, while I was more interested in the horizon. The desolate area around us was the bottom of a once-vast lake. Lifeless rocky hills - previously covered with a forest of ordinary-sized trees - surrounded us. The remains of an industrial road were still visible in front of the tunnel entrance. Judging by the sun barely shining through the brown clouds, the evening was approaching. The wind here was not as strong as expected, and far away, I saw something like a mirage swaying in the haze.

"It can't be!" I said out loud. "Mistassini! Lez, I found water."

"Min Jee," Lez said, his voice hoarse. He stood a little further into the tunnel, bending over some object. "Me too."

He had come across something that resembled a modest picnic. On an overturned plastic box stood a flask with the emblem of a three-string harp, two enamel mugs, and a sandwich container with a couple of flatbreads. There was also a piece of paper, pinned down by a stone, with an arrow pointing into the tunnel and the words, "Come when you feel better. Kir."

"Lez, dear, we're at Île Rouleau. Kir himself found us and brought us here."

"Are you sure it's him, my flower?" Lez asked, pouring two full mugs of water. "This could be a Cruiser's trap."

"Look at the container. It has the Resistance's emblem."

"A musical instrument? What, strings versus brass?" He drank the water in one gulp and poured himself some more.

"Very funny. It symbolises the constellation of Lyra, where our surviving colony is supposed to be. Maiser wanted the remaining people to go there and start over. Mmm. Wow! Even in the new headquarters, water wasn't this good!"

We drank all the water and ate the bread. Still hungry but feeling much better, we ventured further down the tunnel, discussing the differences between the realistic ways to save humanity. It wasn't as dark as it had seemed from the outside, even where it curved. In some places, the famous earthquakes of November 3352 had left huge cracks overhead through which daylight poured. The ground also had cracks, and we finally reached the largest bottomless hole. An intricate vehicle was parked before it, seemingly modified from an old electro-truck. Judging by the panel plates and complex converters on the roof, it ran on ZP energy. No one was inside the truck, but we found our belongings by it - everything except my terminal and the book I had found in the house. Hopefully, they were still safe in the hiding place.

"Where is he?" Lez asked after a happy reunion with his axe, his fingers tightening around the familiar handle.

Before I could respond, a door in the wall we hadn't noticed slid open with a soft hiss. A figure stepped out, not very tall but composed, dressed in a blend of military attire and desert survival gear. A scarf partially obscured their face, leaving only sharp eyes visible.

"Welcome," the figure said in an unexpectedly warm female voice. "You must be Min Jee and Lez Prosser."

Lez and I looked at each other, our guard still up. "Where is Kir Vendy?" Lez asked.

The woman before us paused for a moment.

"Kir Vendy never existed," she said. "You were looking for me. I am Wendy Kir."

Lez's surprise was evident, and I quickly connected the dots. So that's why the Cruisers never found Maiser's elusive assistant. "Clever!" I said aloud, "I would've done the same in your place. Even the rebels gave us a description of a man with the rest of the info. They didn't know either."

"Exactly," the woman replied, uncovering her face. "You can call me Wendy."

Her features were handsome, and she was younger than I expected.

"And I have questions," Lez said, his voice sharp with suspicion. "What happened in Montreal? What were we drugged with? How did we end up here, and why did you leave us at the entrance to the tunnel?"

Wendy sighed, stepping closer. "I was in that house too and saw the Thieves attack you. When it became clear you couldn't handle them, I threw a grenade with a concentrated compound of my own recipe. It's a strong sedative; its only real harm is its side effects. I know it was risky, but you've recovered without needing an antidote. I spared you a dangerous stroll across the desert and brought you and your things in my truck. I left you at the entrance to ensure you weren't Cruisers but rather the couple I was waiting for."

"Ensure how?" Lez asked.

"I listened to your conversations as you walked through the tunnel," Wendy replied. "The microphones and cameras along its entire length are part of my security system. People can easily give themselves away if they think they're alone. A decent person behaves with decency even when no one is watching. Are you ready to come with me?"

"And if we'd been silent?" I asked as I ducked through the low doorway.

Wendy chuckled. "No one is silent when they come to that hole in the floor. Not even those who come without company."

The technical rooms beyond the tunnel walls seemed like a labyrinth. Still, Wendy navigated them with ease, her steps confident and sure. We followed closely behind, and Lez leaned in and whispered in my ear, "Min, do you think this woman could've picked me up unconscious by herself, carried me out of that house, and loaded me into the car?"

I had wondered the same, but before I could respond, we reached another door. Bright light spilled out as it opened, almost blinding after the dim corridors we had passed through.

"Welcome to the Cave of Hope," Wendy said, gesturing for us to enter. "We can talk here."

The built-in cave facility was well-lit and domesticated, a cool and inviting refuge starkly contrasting with the dusty, oppressive tunnels we had just traversed. Maps lined the walls, screens streamed endless data, and shelves were neatly stacked with supplies. In the centre of the room, a small table held a decent spread of food and water – a sight that made my stomach rumble.

Wendy noticed and gave a slight nod, gesturing for us to sit. "Help yourselves. It's safe."

Lez and I exchanged wary glances before cautiously taking our seats. As we began to eat, Wendy sat across from us, her gaze fixed intently on our faces.

"I know you've been through a lot to get here," she said, her tone softer now, almost sympathetic. "Help me understand why you went through so much trouble to find me."

Lez paused mid-bite and looked up. "You don't know?"

"I know you're not just ramblers," Wendy replied, leaning forward. "You rebel against sects and look for something most people have given up on. But what do you want from me? Vatslav Maiser is dead, his staff scattered, and his work was destroyed to keep it out of the Cruisers' hands. His last acolyte and I might be the last of his assistants, trying to survive, too."

I set the half-eaten pie back on the platter and met her gaze. "You're trying to survive here when you could have stayed on Mars, where the Cruisers haven't dared go since the raid on the cargo fleet. The Resort of Hope isn't just a place – it's an idea, a last chance for those who refuse to give up. I'm convinced you have a good reason for being here, but you're not with the Resistance. Why?"

"You came to recruit me?" Wendy asked, raising an eyebrow.

"You should be leading it," Lez said.

"No, Lez." I corrected him gently. "Wendy is a scientist, not a leader. She might be the only one to continue Maiser's work and help us find the last loader."

Wendy leaned back, studying us. "To what end?"

I sighed, feeling the weight of our mission. "The Cruisers are moving fast. They're brainwashing people into relocating to the moon's cryogenic tanks - or worse - drifting into space, praying for salvation by a godly entity. Many choose this path because they think it's easier than resurrecting the Object mission. But the Resistance hasn't given up hope. We believe we can travel through wormholes again. The ships can still be built."

Wendy nodded thoughtfully. "In theory, yes. But why do you need a loader? Are you sure you can't do it without one?"

"It's not that we can't," I said. "Many have fought against the odds, believing there's a way to survive on different planets. But time is running out. A loader could accelerate our success, saving more good lives along the way."

Wendy's expression hardened. "What do you know about loaders? Do you even understand how they were created?"

I took a deep breath. "Yes. Loaders were artificially bred to integrate with neuroware, vastly enhancing their knowledge and abilities. One loader can do the work of hundreds of trained individuals. But we don't have the time or resources to train those hundreds, and we're fighting against Cruisers, too."

Wendy frowned, her eyes narrowing. "Do you know how many clones died in the process? How many didn't make it to their fifth birthday? The implants and tissue transplants sometimes exceeded the original organism. Even when some survived the build, the overloading fried what was left of their brain cells. It's as if they were bred to be intellectual slaves, although for a noble purpose. If I were a loader, I'd hide too – to ensure neither the Cruisers nor the Resistance could use me. That loader has nothing to gain from helping us."

The room fell into a heavy silence, the weight of her words pressing down on us.

"So there *is* a survivor," Lez said slowly.

"There is. I've heard you wanted to find and protect the last one," Wendy replied.

"Yes," I confirmed. "Do you know which of the twins still lives?"

Wendy shook her head. "I can't tell. I care too, you know. Some exterminated loaders were my friends. But if you want to protect the last one, let them be. That loader might eventually agree to help – if we show them we are committed to helping ourselves. Promise me not to seek them any longer, and I'll help you build the wormhole ships."

Lez resumed eating. I sat still, processing the shift in our mission. It wasn't the outcome I had hoped for, but it was something – a way forward.

Finally, I broke the silence. "What do you need us to do?"

Wendy's smile was warm once again, her eyes revealing nothing. "First, you rest. I need to think. Then we'll talk about what comes next."

6. 21/12/3406

Lez woke me in the middle of the night, his eyes wide with excitement. A true love machine . . . but no. He was dressed, his movements tense with urgency.

"Quiet," he whispered, gesturing for me to follow. "It turns out our Miss Kir doesn't live here alone."

We slipped out of the room that had served as our temporary bedroom, moving silently across the central hall of the cave. Lez led me to a spiral staircase that descended into the depths of the facility. As we crept down, the faint murmur of voices reached us from below. We halted just above where the steps ended, straining to hear the conversation.

Two men were speaking. One voice was youthful; the other, older, had a distinct

Eastern accent.

"I am glad you are still willing, but don't worry *too* much about us," the younger voice said. "Tell me about your wife and children instead."

"What is there to tell?" replied the older man. "Citta is ageing, though not as quickly as I am. Both our daughters are married now. Rodion's busy inventing something again, always tinkering. It's a pity I'll never see grandchildren."

"You might not see them, but at least you could have them if you help us," the young man said.

"You can't promise me that."

The younger man sighed. "You're right. Okay then. Until next time – if you access the MESH next week."

"Until next time," the older man replied.

A soft beep indicated a disconnection

from the MESH, followed by the soft rustling of some loose clothing. Lez and I crept back to our room, our minds racing.

"Are you thinking what I'm thinking?" I asked once we were safely inside.

"Wendy's hiding the loader here, in these facilities," Lez said.

"A loader could easily have carried a biomass like you out of those ruins," I said, recalling how we had speculated about the mysterious rescue.

"What are we going to do?" Lez asked.

"Nothing," I replied firmly. "We must respect their decision. We swore an oath to protect the loader. Wendy is right - if he doesn't want to help humanity, then no amount of persuasion or torture by the Cruisers will change that, especially after everything he's been through."

"But, Min—" Lez began.

"No, Lez." I cut him off gently. "Go back to sleep. Tomorrow promises to be interesting."

Lez hesitated, then nodded, his shoulders relaxing as he accepted my decision. We settled back into our beds, but sleep didn't come easily. My mind was a whirl of thoughts – of the loader, Wendy, and what the future might hold.

7. 21/12/3406

In the morning, Wendy waited for us at the table set for breakfast. We savoured real macchiato and fresh buns with sandie-pâté for the first time in two years. The rich aroma of the coffee and the warmth of the freshly baked bread made me momentarily forget where we were. Breakfast was a silent affair, with neither Lez nor I daring to break the calm with questions. However, I could see the curiosity burning in Lez's eyes.

After breakfast, Wendy dropped a bomb. "Have you heard of the Ruslan Baker from the British Peninsula?" she asked, her tone serious.

Lez answered, "Who hasn't? Thanks to his inventions, agriculture and livestock farming still exist on Earth."

"I know Ruslan and his family well," Wendy continued. "Vatslav Maiser was his teacher, and we collaborated on various projects. Baker can build the ship we need, but I must return to Mars to enable him. Vatslav's work, which is hidden there, is crucial for the project. Will you fly with me? My new capsule has room for three."

Lez and I replied in unison: "Yes." Although it was hard. Knowing the loader was likely hidden nearby, we had to honour our commitment. A deal was a deal. Also, this place was a rare treat, with its cool temperatures, good food and excellent shower room. But the prospect of a more interesting adventure ahead quickly quelled my reluctance.

"Great," Wendy said, standing up. "Get ready. We leave in half an hour."

Our departure was a shock. We found ourselves standing at the edge of a black hole in the ground, the same one Wendy's truck was parked near when we first arrived. Dressed for the road, we entered the tunnel through the same door, though the atmosphere felt different now - tenser, more foreboding. Wendy picked up a stone from the ground and tossed it into the hole. It vanished into the darkness without a sound.

She got behind the wheel and directed the truck towards the hole at an alarming speed. My heart pounded in my chest, and I froze in terror while Lez, always more impulsive, screamed.

But instead of plunging into the abyss, the truck continued smoothly, as if driving on a solid road. Wendy stopped the vehicle and snapped her fingers. The black abyss beneath us disappeared, revealing a perfectly serviceable, though cracked, road.

Finally finding my voice, I asked hoarsely, "Is that another part of the security system?"

"Precisely," Wendy replied with a slight smile. "A hologram. This tunnel will take us to the Spaceport of Hope, where the builders of the KOSI station in Jupiter's orbit launched and where the first colonists began their journey during the Platinum Age, a thousand years ago. Maiser started building ships that could reach the colony in the Lyra constellation within weeks instead of decades. But we had to destroy them when the Cruisers kidnapped and killed him. I managed to save the blueprints on Mars. When you deliver them to Baker, no one should know where they came from - not even his son. I don't want Cruisers' attention to the colony again. Do you understand?"

"Certainly."

"Are you going to stay on Mars?" Lez asked with a frown.

"Yes," Wendy said. "I'll be more useful there. Trust me."

We left the tunnel and drove through an empty city that had clearly been untouched by human hands for years. It wasn't vandalised or looted. The windows of shops and cafes were still intact, samples of forgotten goods visible in the display cases, the wind-beaten canvas awnings not torn off. The sight of empty front gardens with benches and abandoned toys added to the ghostly atmosphere.

We drove out of the city and across a large concrete flatland, searching for the secret hatch leading to a hidden shaft where critical equipment and a space vessel awaited us. But we never made it to the hatch.

Wendy suddenly stopped the truck and stepped out, her body tense as she listened intently.

"What's wrong?" Lez asked.

"Quiet," Wendy said with a hiss, shading her eyes with one hand as she scanned the south-eastern horizon.

I strained my ears and heard it, too – a faint, growing buzz. Dark dots appeared on the horizon, growing larger and revealing themselves as old-fashioned thermocopters. I had heard rumours that the Cruisers raided military museums all over the planet, but seeing these relics in action was something else entirely.

The thermocopters circled above us, landing one by one, forming an inescapable ring. We could not outrun them in the truck; they were too fast.

The insignias on the boards were unmistakable - Cruisers, but not Mooners. These belonged to the Moses Movement. The symbol - a fish standing on its tail, resembling a missile - was a chilling reminder of their fanaticism.

Figures in sky-blue robes armed with clubs and axes poured out of the antique vessels, running towards us. Among them, a tall man in a dark blue robe walked slowly, confidently, holding a twenty-second-century firearm - an old relic, yet deadly. A zapper is a useless weapon when the enemy surrounds you in all directions. So I gripped my lance, ready to fight.

Lez's voice trembled as he whispered, "Oh no . . . Father Sebastian. The unloader."

The man's eyes met Lez's, a twisted smile forming on his lips.

"Hello, Brother Lezoraz!" Father Sebastian called out, his voice mock-friendly. "I see you've picked up a couple of tasty ladies since we last saw each other. Thank you for leading us here." He turned to his men and ordered, "Disarm them."

Before I could react, strong hands clamped down on my shoulders, pinning me in place. Wendy, unarmed, watched as our axes, blades and spears were swiftly taken away. My mind raced, struggling to comprehend what was happening. I turned to Lez in disbelief, but he looked just as lost as I felt.

Father Sebastian spoke again, "Don't worry, Mrs Prosser. Your husband didn't betray you. He forgot that the Lord's watchful eye never lets His flock stray far."

Wendy's eyes narrowed. "If your husband is a former Cruiser, he probably has a tracker under his skin he wasn't even aware of," she said coldly. "I should have checked."

Father Sebastian sneered. "So, where is the loader you were looking for, Lez?" he demanded, pointing his gun directly at Wendy. "Since you entered the resort, we expected you would find him. Where is he, Lezoraz? Answer me."

Lez's voice wavered as he responded, "We didn't find him."

The world seemed to slow down. Without hesitation, Father Sebastian pulled the trigger. The gunshot echoed like thunder. Wendy, who had been standing beside me just moments ago - a living, breathing woman, possibly the most important person on Earth - now lay face down on the weathered concrete.

I stared in horror, my mind refusing to accept what had happened. The cold barrel of Father Sebastian's gun was now aimed at me. "Where is the loader, Lez? Have you forgotten why you were born into this world? You're here to serve the Lord and those He has marked with His blessing."

"Don't shoot!" Lez shouted, his voice breaking. Tears welled up in his eyes; the strongest, bravest man I knew was reduced to a terrified child in that moment. His only weakness had been exposed – me.

The circle of men tightened around us, their breath heavy with the stench of worm stew. They grinned, relishing the spectacle, their eyes gleaming.

Father Sebastian now spoke like a preacher. "Because of such blasphemers, this planet is turning into a piece of shit incapable of supporting life. The Lord wants to save His children, but even here, you try to stand in His way. You know how much I dislike mess and disorder, Lezoraz, but you leave me no choice. Your wife is so sweet. You don't want to lose her over that man. But what am I saying? The loader isn't a man; he's an affront to everything holy and righteous." And then he added coldly, "I'm asking you for the last time, Brother Lezoraz. Where is the loader?"

Lez's gaze darted to me, filled with panic and guilt. "Forgive me," he said, then turned to Father Sebastian.

My husband, my love and best friend opened his mouth to speak, ready to reveal the last loader's location in the desperate hope they would spare me. Why? He told me many times that unloaders never spared hostages. We were both already dead.

In one swift motion, I pulled back my sleeve and activated my zapper. A short, bright ray pierced Lez's body, making his clothes smoulder.

"I'm sorry," I whispered, apologising to the doomed world for my failure.

Lez collapsed to the ground, gasping for breath, his hand clutching the wound. I dropped to my knees beside him, cradling his head. "Thank you, my flower," he whispered, his voice barely audible. "I love you."

"I love you too," I said, my voice breaking.

A calculating coldness replaced Father Sebastian's amusement. He opened fire again.

"Bitch!" he spat, his voice filled with venom. Then he turned and signalled his men to retreat. A minute later, they were all gone. Around us, there was only the horizon – flat and empty.

At first, I didn't realise that I had been shot. The physical pain felt distant, insignificant compared to the agony of losing Lez. The world around me blurred – the fight, the cause, everything we had fought for – slipping away as my life drained.

"Lez!" I called out, my voice weak and trembling. His eyelids fluttered slightly; he could hear me, but only a groan escaped his lips. His grip on life was loosening, and there was nothing I could do.

We were bleeding out alone in this concrete desert. But why was it taking so long for us to die?

A soft noise behind me drew my attention, pulling me from the brink of sorrow. With great effort, I lifted my head. Wendy stood over me, alive, pressing her hand to the wound on her throat, blood seeping through her fingers. But something about her was different – her entire demeanour had shifted. Her face was distorted with pain.

"You're alive!" I managed to whisper, my voice fading as the darkness closed in. "Looks like we're not going to Mars after all."

"I'm so sorry," Wendy replied. Her voice sounded wrong – metallic and damaged, neither male nor female. My mind was slipping away, but for a brief moment, I thought I saw not Wendy but someone else standing over me – a young man, perhaps, or a woman with a pale and tired face. The death itself? Was I hallucinating? This person pulled off their headscarf, revealing a half-shaved head and a mass of copper-red hair that lifted slightly in the breeze. With one hand, they pressed the scarf to my wound, trying to stem the flow of blood. But it was too late.

"Oh, I see . . ." I muttered, my vision blurring. "You know, Mr Loader . . . I wish I believed in the afterlife . . . for the comfort of the hope of meeting Lez there."

The metallic voice responded, "I can do . . . I will make sure you are always together."

I coughed weakly, lowering my head onto Lez's chest.

"Hah . . . Can you hear that, my love? Wouldn't that be nice?" I whispered. "Thank you, Wendy . . . or whoever you are."

"My name is Vist," was the last thing I heard.

The last thing I saw was the bloody hand on Lez's forehead. The last thing I felt was the hot fingers on mine. Then I felt nothing. A second later . . . I died.

8. 25/12/3406

The wind on the streets of Montreal felt familiar, like an old companion. It swept through the deserted streets, stirring up litter that danced in the air – the remnants of a world that had long since faded. Once vibrant and alive, the city now stood quiet, its silence broken only by the rustling of plastic waste and the occasional creak of an abandoned building.

A solitary figure emerged from one of the crumbling doorways, draped in a broad hooded robe that concealed their features. They held a worn book, its pages yellowed with age. The figure paused, glancing down at the object in their hands.

"Happy Christmas. Nice one, my flower!" the person murmured, their voice carrying a strange metallic undertone that seemed to blend with the wind. The words were soft, almost reverent, as if spoken to someone dear.

The figure began to walk slowly, its form gradually fading into the swirling dust and the shadows that filled the streets.

To be continued …

Thank you for finishing this book. The author would greatly appreciate an honest review if you're willing. Thank you again!

Book 1 Object & Vist, (a Trailer):

The bald, still young, but weathered man touched his bleeding lip with his tongue and waited for the next question.

"Five years ago, the unauthorised vessel WSP-41 performed a shift to Earth's only known colony in the constellation of Lyra. Was it you who was in command of that vessel?"

"Yes."

"On whose orders?"

"It was not an official trip. It was a decision agreed by many."

"What do you call your group? Do you work for the Resistance?"

"I never liked that name. We are the part of the human population who don't want to take blind chances."

"Careful, Captain. Blasphemy is not welcomed here."

"But sins are?"

The next punch was even more painful than the one before. The twisted bastard was aiming at the same spot, which was already raw and tender.

"My hand is guided by my Lord, you … wretched man! To show you the right way, any means are good means!" A big, muscular Cruiser in a sky-blue hooded robe stood up straight and smiled, "But it is sinful for you to hit me back. That would be an act of malevolence. Now, tell me, why did you stop by Mars before you opened the wormhole for a shift?"

He took a few steps back and stared at Tom expectantly. Tom realised that he had been given a few seconds to compose himself. He squinted past the candles and tried to look around. We are not outside, he thought, but rather inside something big. The voices echo. It's not a cave. He dropped his head and briefly examined the tiled floor. A large hall … or a cathedral? He tried to make out the walls, but the darkness swallowed them. A group of small candles failed to show anything useful. But Tom could not stop feeling that there was something important there, not far away.

"Time to answer," said the Cruiser and stepped closer, bringing his sweaty stench with him.

"We had to pick up a package."

"What was in the package?"

"Essential equipment."

"Do you want me to hit you again? We know you picked up a person."

"The equipment comes with an operator."

"Who was that operator?"

Thomas Darkwood sighed. They already knew. "Look, you can smash my face into mince if you like. I can't tell you much, even if I wanted to. This "operator" was a weird one – they kept away from everyone and did not speak much. I thought at first that it was synthetic. I mean … really. Just imagine, it didn't need a medic to rise from the pod, it could access the entire database, it consumed minimum rations, and I don't think it slept at all."

"But it was not a synth," the Cruiser confirmed, before continuing. "Nobody builds synths anymore. For centuries they failed to produce synthetic life that would last a year. They're expensive and unreliable junk."

"No. This one was definitely a human. One of those who doesn't want to be known by other people."

"But who was it? Was it a man or a woman?"

"I don't know!" This was said with such strong emotion that the Cruiser surprised himself by believing this sinner.

"Hmm. We suspect they were a loader. We really could do with one. And the name? Surely they introduced themself."

The pause was too long to be polite.

"Vist."

ABOUT THE AUTHOR

Anka B. Troitsky, a multi-award-winning author and philosopher, came to the UK from Kazakhstan in 1993. With a rich background as a science teacher, translator of books, legal cases and NHS interpreter, she channels her diverse experiences and insights into the science fiction genre, exploring the depths of what she has learned and understood throughout her journey.

Subscribe for an Email list: www.ankatroitsky.com

Novels:

- OBJECT & VIST
- CONSTRUCT & VIST
- VIST & PROPER GANDA
- WHO WAS VIST

Part in Anthology:

- 2024 Next Generation Short Story Awards Anthology of Winners
- Borne in the Blood
- The Dragon's Hoard 2

Printed in Great Britain
by Amazon

46418797R00051